For my cousins and our shared memories of Paul—P.C.

First American Edition 2018
Kane Miller, A Division of EDC Publishing

Text copyright © Phil Cummings, 2017
Illustrations copyright © Shane Devries, 2017

First published by Scholastic Press, a division of Scholastic Australia Pty Limited in 2017
This edition published under license from Scholastic Australia Pty Limited

For information contact:
Kane Miller, A Division of EDC Publishing
PO Box 470663
Tulsa, OK 74147-0663
www.kanemiller.com
www.usbornebooksandmore.com
www.edcpub.com

Library of Congress Control Number: 2017942430

Printed in China
1 2 3 4 5 6 7 8 9 10

ISBN: 978-1-61067-739-4

BOY

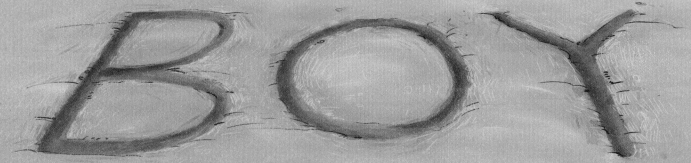

PHIL CUMMINGS   SHANE DEVRIES

Kane Miller
A DIVISION OF EDC PUBLISHING

Once there was a king who lived high on a hill. His castle looked over the valley to the mountains beyond.

He was a powerful man with many brave knights.

The mountains were once rich with trees,
but a powerful dragon had destroyed much
of the forest with his fiery breath.

In a small village on the edge of the burned forest lived Boy.

Boy couldn't hear, but he was happy. He spoke with dancing hands and he drew pictures for people in the sand.

His parents loved his stories . . .

but the villagers didn't understand.

"What a strange child," they would say as they walked by.

Since the forest had been burned,

the king and the dragon had fought many fierce battles.

There was roaring,

flapping,

running around,

hiding,

dodging,

weaving

and a lot of shouting.

AARGE!

tiNG

tiNG!

Boy couldn't hear the battle cries, but he had
seen the fear in his mother's eyes and felt it
in his father's hands when he held him close.

The battles were loud and long . . .

but no one ever won.

One day, when the king and the dragon
were battling once more . . .

ROAr
ROaAaR
ROA

CLiNG
CLANG
TiNG

Boy ran right into the middle of it all.

The knights were stunned. "MOVE!" they shouted.

"GET OUT OF THE WAY, BOY!" ordered the king.

"ROAR!" bellowed the dragon.

But, of course, Boy couldn't hear them.

Flames flared from the dragon's nostrils.

HISSSSSS
HISSSSS!

CLANK!

The knights waved their swords frantically
as they marched over to Boy.

CLiNG
CLONG
CLANG!

"Why aren't you listening?" shouted the king.

Boy was surprised when he looked up
and saw them all. He watched them for
a moment, then made his hands dance.

The knights were flabbergasted.
The king was puzzled.
The dragon was mystified.

Boy could see that they didn't understand him,
so he took a sword and wrote in the sand.

WHY ARE YOU

There was silence until . . .

Suddenly the king pointed to the
dragon. "He started it!" he cried.
"He burned our forest!"

The dragon shook his head. "It was an accident," he
roared. "I sneezed a fireball into the trees. I came to say
sorry, but your knights chased me away!"

The knights pointed to the king. "He told us to," they cried.

The king looked up at the dragon. "Well, I thought you were coming to take my castle," he said.

"Your castle is far too small for me," the dragon replied.

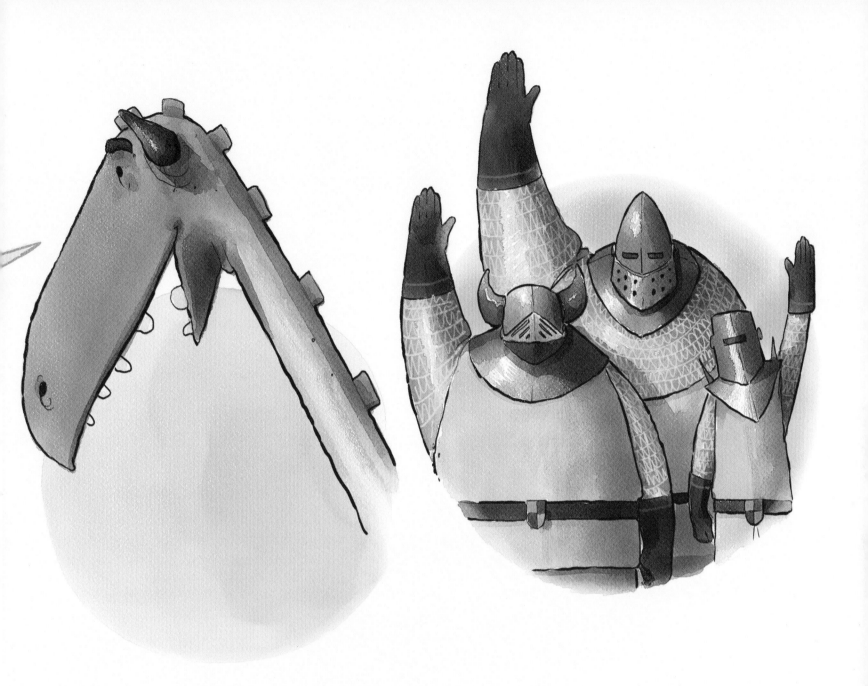

"All I want is for you to stop chasing me. I don't like being scared."

"Nor do we," chorused the knights.

Boy drew a picture of everyone in the sand.

He showed them how their days could be,
without fighting and fear.

There was a lot of chatting and laughing.

"I promise the knights won't chase you anymore," said the king to the dragon. "And you can visit my castle whenever you like."

"And I will cover my nose when I sneeze," said the dragon.

Boy couldn't hear a word, but he didn't need to.

Back in the village,

everyone was waiting to see Boy . . .

(thank you)

(thank you)

(thank you)

(thank you)

(thank you)

"Thank you," they said with dancing hands.